For Jeffrey, Hilda, and Frank,
with thanks and love.
—J. L.

To my husband Sal,
a wonderful new father.
—L. C.

Library of Congress Cataloging-in-Publication Data
Lawler, Janet.
A father's song / Janet Lawler; illustrated by Lucy Corvino.
p.   cm.
Summary: A father and child react to one another with delight as they play together.
ISBN 1-4027-2501-9
[1. Father and child—Fiction. 2. Stories in rhyme.] I. Corvino, Lucy, ill. II. Title.
PZ8.3.L355Far 2006   [E]—dc22   2005019127

2   4   6   8   10   9   7   5   3   1

Published by Sterling Publishing Co., Inc.
387 Park Avenue South, New York, NY 10016
Text copyright © 2006 by Janet Lawler
Illustrations copyright © 2006 by Lucy Corvino
Distributed in Canada by Sterling Publishing
c/o Canadian Manda Group, 165 Dufferin Street
Toronto, Ontario, Canada M6K 3H6
Distributed in Great Britain and Europe by Chris Lloyd at Orca Book
Services, Stanley House, Fleets Lane, Poole BH15 3AJ, England
Distributed in Australia by Capricorn Link (Australia) Pty. Ltd.
P.O. Box 704, Windsor, NSW 2756, Australia
Printed in China. All rights reserved.
Sterling ISBN 1-4027-2501-9

For information about custom editions, special sales, premium and
corporate purchases, please contact Sterling Special Sales
Department at 800-805-5489 or specialsales@sterlingpub.com.

A Father's Song

A Father's Song

By *Janet Lawler*

Illustrated by Lucy Corvino

Sterling Publishing Co., Inc.

New York

If I lift you up high
on my shoulders to see,
the view becomes better
for both you and me.

If I gather you close
as we zoom down the slide,
you squeal with delight
as we go on our ride.

If I roar like a bear
coming out of its cave,
you growl in reply
just to show me you're brave.

If I chase you around
playing tag through the trees,
you laugh when I catch you
and give you a squeeze.

If I scrunch up my face
as you're starting to cry,
your tears turn to giggles
before your eyes dry.

If I squeak like a mouse
or I bark like a hound,
you clap right along
and make each silly sound.

If I fly you around
like an airplane that swoops,
you spread out your wings,
making wide loop-de-loops.

If I push so the swing arcs
as high as it goes,
you reach for the sky
when you kick up your toes.

If I wade in the water
and swirl you about,
you splash in the waves
as you giggle and shout.

I can lift you and squeeze you
and fly all day long,
to bring on your laughter,
as sweet as a song.

And I'll carry you home
in my arms' warm embrace
to show you my love,
any time, any place.

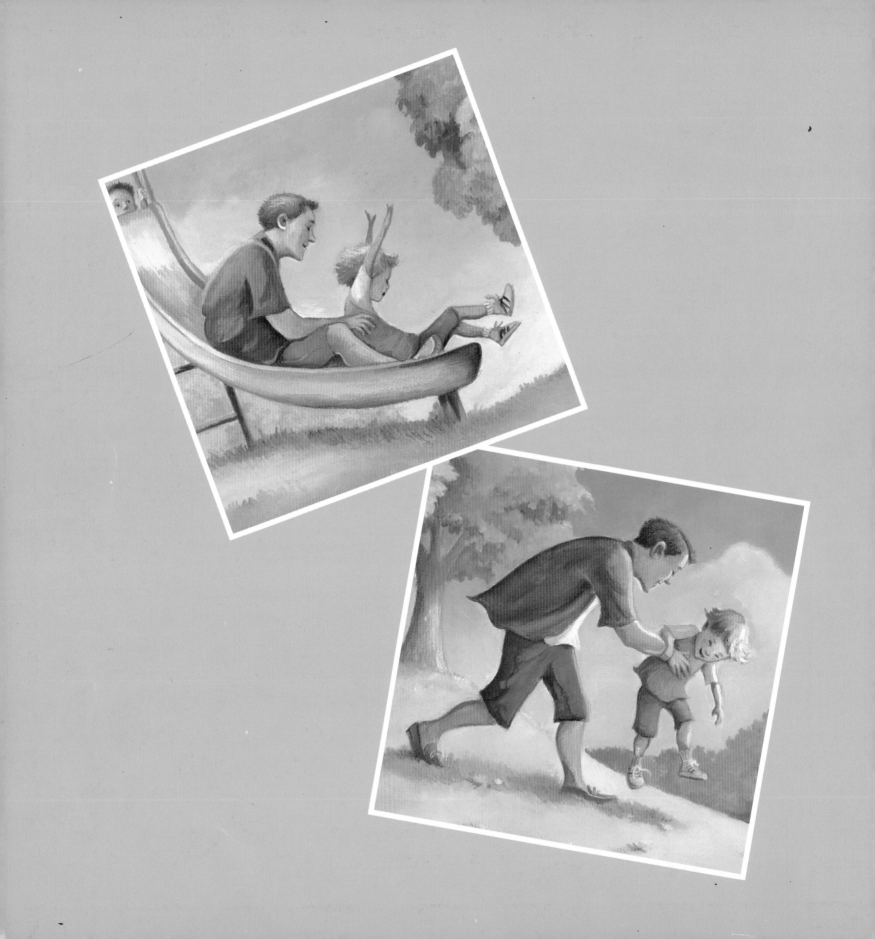